This book is dedicated to...
My kids...Mariah, Michael, Marshall, & Miles
My hubby...Mike
My guardian angels...Geraldine & Martha
&
All of the children out there with a sparkly imagination,
big dreams, and loose teeth (wink)

Written by Kimesha Malone, RN
Illustrated by Claudia L. Munoz
Edited by Shannon Jade, Wildflower Books
Printed in China

Library of Congress Cataloging-in-Publication data available

www.yomamasworld.com

SANTA MEETS THE TOOTH FAIRY

Once upon a time, there was a peppermint-scented fairy named Tairy. She was known for her fashionable outfits, fun glasses, and fancy accessories.

Tairy the Fairy used to work at the North Pole as an elf in the Department of Toy Quality Control. She NEVER got the chance to see Santa in person.

After a few years, elves earned their wings and got new jobs.

Tairy's friend Troy went on to be a Fairy Godfather.
Kim-Lavender became a Wedding Fairy.

Tairy's best buddy became a big star
in cartoon movies.

Tairy graduated and got promoted to
Tooth Fairy!

After Halloween, Tairy's new job kept her very busy.
Kids eating lots of treats and hard candy meant
that there was plenty of work for Tairy.

On Christmas Eve, a boy named Miles had a loose tooth.

He wiggled it and wiggled it. He jiggled it and jiggled it.

Then . . . **BOOM!** It came out.

"Mom! Dad! My tooth fell out!" Miles yelled.

"Oh dear!" Miles's mom said. "It sure did. Here's a cup of salt water to rinse your mouth out with and a special holder to place your tooth in."

He placed the tooth in the holder, brushed his teeth, and rinsed his mouth.

Miles put the holder under his pillow and fell fast asleep.

Tairy's fairy phone soon buzzed with a text message.

This was Tairy's first time delivering on a holiday. "Oh boy!" she said. "My first Christmas Eve delivery! I'm so excited!" She grabbed her gift bag, which was filled with money and glitter.

Then, she flew out into the night.

Tairy arrived at Miles's house at midnight. It was very
windy and snowy outside. She heard a loud

BUMP!

She hurried through the window.

The wind blew so hard that it pushed Tairy into the house and onto the floor. She looked up and saw a big, blurry red snowball coming toward her.

She tried to run, but it was too late.

BOOM!

Fairy dust, snow, and teeth went everywhere.

Tairy shook the snow out of her hair, fixed her glasses, and looked up. "Santa?"

Santa stared back at her.

"You know who I am?" Tairy asked.

Santa replied with a chuckle. "Ho! Ho! Of course! You were our best elf."

"Wow! It's so nice to *finally* meet you!" Tairy replied.

They laughed and chatted about memories from the North Pole until...they heard the sound of footsteps.

They rushed to pick everything up off the floor.

Tairy disappeared, and Santa dashed back up the chimney.

Miles had awakened.

He looked under his pillow, and to his surprise, he found ten dollars!
"Wow!" he shouted. "I heard that if you lose your tooth on Christmas
Eve, you get double. And it's true!"

He woke his parents up and ran down the steps to see what goodies Santa had brought.

Miles yelled, "Mom! Dad! Wake up! It's Christmas!"

As he knelt down in front of the tree, Miles shouted,

"This is the best Christmas ever! I got money from the Tooth Fairy **AND** gifts from Santa!"

WHOOOOOOOO-HOOOOOOOO!!!

Miles's older brother, Michael, grabbed *his* tooth. "I think I'm next," he said. "See! Look at it jiggle."

"Uh-uh!" Michael's twin brother, Marshall, replied.
"Mine is next. See! Look at it wiggle."

They went back and forth until their older sister, Mariah, entered the room, rubbing her eyes.
"Stop it, guys!" she ordered.

It's too early to be fussing. Plus, it's Christmas! Let's just open our presents so I can get back to resting my beautiful eyes.

The family was still sleepy from waking up so early to open gifts, so they headed back to bed for a little snooze.

As Miles and his siblings climbed up the stairs, Miles looked down and noticed something.

He stopped his brothers and sister. "Guys," he said. "The tooth fairy took *my* tooth, but whose is this?"

Tairy looked out of her window and into the sky.
She spotted Santa flying by.

Tairy waved goodbye.

As Tairy got ready for bed, her fairy phone buzzed.
She let out a giggle.
"See you tomorrow, Santa!"

"Merry Christmas, Tairy! Ho ho ho!"